THE LUCKIEST ONE OF ALL

OF ALL BILL PEET

Houghton Mifflin Company   Boston

With Gratitude
to the
John Herron Art Institute
at Indianapolis

Library of Congress Cataloging in Publication Data
Peet, Bill.
The luckiest one of all.
Summary: Wishing to be a bird, a little boy learns
that there are benefits and drawbacks to every condi-
tion and that being a little boy may be the best of all.

[1. Self-acceptance—Fiction. 2. Stories in rhyme]
I. Title.
PZ8.3.P2764Lu: [E]   81-7094
   ISBN 0-395-31863-7   AACR2

Printed in the United States of America

ISBN 0-395-31863-7 Reinforced Edition
ISBN 0-395-39593-3 Sandpiper Paperbound Edition

Y 10 9 8 7 6 5

"There are so many things I'd much rather be,"
Said a boy sitting up in a sycamore tree,
"And I wish I knew of some magical word
That would suddenly change me into a bird.
What a terrific treat it would be to go flying
High over the tree tops without even half trying!
Of all the wild creatures the bird is the one
Who seems to be having most of the fun."

"I seldom have fun," chirped a brown speckled thrush;
"I'm always caught up in a last-minute rush.
There's a nest I must build, and then eggs to hatch,
And for lunch I've got to find insects to catch;
I go chasing about in the stormiest weather,
Drenched and bedraggled to the very last feather.
If I were given a choice to be just what I wish
Then I'd gladly trade places with a lazy ole fish."

"Don't envy poor me," said a calico bass;
"I'm always in danger, alack and alas—
I must watch what I eat, just to make sure
I don't get hooked on a fisherman's lure,
And no matter how big I happen to be
There is always a bigger fish looking for me.
The turtle's the one who's got it all made
He's safe in his shell, and is never afraid."

"Being safe," said the turtle, "is all very well,
But it gets pretty tiresome toting this shell.
And I'm also fed up with being a joke,
With everyone calling me Mister Slowpoke;
And if I could trade this cumbersome shell of mine
For a pair of frog legs, I would get along fine.
I'd love to be bouncy and light on my feet—
To jump like a bullfrog would be a rare treat."

"It's just great," said the frog, "to be able to jump,
But I'm not at all pleased with my old jugger-rump.
If I had my way and were given a choice,
And I could pick another sound for my voice,
I would much prefer to hoot like an owl,
Or sound like a wolf and cut loose with a howl.
And if I were a lion with a thundering roar,
Then I would never wish to be anything more."

"I roar," said the lion who lived in the zoo,
"Just to pass the time and have something to do.
But if I roar too long or a little too loud,
I'm sure to attract an inquisitive crowd.

They run up to my cage and stare through the bars
As if I were some freaky creature from Mars.
If I were a gopher, I'd be gone in a minute—
I'd dig a deep hole, then hide myself in it."

The gopher said, "I dig myself out of sight
To avoid being caught out in broad daylight.
I dig with a frenzy and for all I'm worth
To make lots of tunnels and holes in the earth.
But I often wish I were a thousand times bigger—
Then, perhaps, I would be a much better digger.
I wish I could be a huge digging machine
Like one of those giant steam shovels I've seen."

The huge steam shovel said, "I *hate* digging deep holes;
Such miserable work is for gophers and moles!
My only reward for this back-breaking toil
Is some grease in my joints and a few squirts of oil.
And if anyone should happen to ask,
I would prefer a much easier task.
The street lamp on the corner has it easy as pie
With nothing to do but watch the people go by."

9

"It's a shame," said the street lamp, "and also a pity,
That I'm stuck right here in the midst of the city.
My brightness is wasted in the glitter and glare
Of a hundred street signs flashing on everywhere.
If it weren't for the moths that visit me nightly,
No one would notice how I glitter so brightly.
I envy the lighthouse so stately and tall,
Whose light is so powerful it outshines them all."

"I'm proud," said the lighthouse, "but I don't mean to boast
When I say my light is more important than most—
My powerful beacon that flashes around
Has saved many a ship from running aground.

But it gets pretty spooky living out here
In this swirling fog and the weird atmosphere.
The great ocean liner is the luckiest one;
Those long pleasure cruises must be wonderful fun."

"That wonderful fun never does include me,"
Grumped the ocean liner plowing through the rough sea.
"Up above on my decks, wild parties go on
Far into the night and into the dawn.

While I must battle the rambunctious ocean
Caught up in a furious, frothing commotion,
I'd much rather be a tall building somewhere
And stand high and dry in a big city square."

15

"I have my own ocean," said a downtown hotel;
"It's a great sea of traffic rushing pell-mell.
There is always a hubbub in the center of town—
All day and all night, and it never calms down.
With the buses roaring and taxicabs beeping,
It's no wonder people have such trouble sleeping.
The life of a barn is what would suit me,
Way out on a farm where it's still as can be."

"Sometimes it's entirely *too* peaceful and still,"
Complained an old barn all alone on a hill.
"So quiet you can hear moss growing on trees,
A butterfly sigh or a grasshopper sneeze.

Out here in the country, life is too slow;
I'd like some excitement and to be on the go.
And if ever the choice were left up to me,
A big diesel truck is what I'd rather be."

"I love going places," said the big diesel truck;
"To be able to travel is wonderful luck.
And I'd feel like the luckiest thing on ten wheels
If it weren't for the impudent automobiles!

They swarm the highway by the hundreds each day,
And they all seem determined to get in my way.
To be a big locomotive is my favorite dream—
With a track to myself and always going full steam."

"If the track were all mine, I'd never complain,"
Said the steam locomotive pulling the train.
"But I have these lumbering boxcars to haul,
Which is one big hassle and no fun at all.
For years I have traveled these very same tracks
Without a day off to slow down and relax,
While the lazy caboose has nothing to do
But come tagging along to enjoy the nice view."

"I've got a fine view," the caboose said, with a sigh,
"If you call clouds of train smoke a treat for the eye!
When I do get a glimpse through the smoke now and then,
It's a backward peek at where I've just been.
And if wishing real hard would be any use,
I'd choose to be anything but a caboose.
My first choice would be a big jumbo jet—
The view from up there is terrific, I'll bet."

"At this height," said the jet, "and as fast as I go,
There is not very much one can see down below.
The rivers appear to be tiny silk threads,
The patches of farmland like quilted bedspreads.

Speed is the thing on these cross-country flights,
With no time to enjoy the beautiful sights.
I'd much rather be a big cloud, if you please,
And go drifting off on a soft, gentle breeze."

"Those soft gentle breezes," complained a big cloud,
"Can get pushy and rude, for cryin' out loud!
They can blow up a storm before I can say *boo*,
And ker-whoosh me from Oshkosh to Kalamazoo.

The day after tomorrow, who knows where I'll be?
I might end up a thousand miles out to sea.
I'd like to stop drifting and stay put for a change,
Like a huge rocky peak on a great mountain range."

The mountain peak muttered, "I've had to stay put
For millions of years without budging one foot—
And I wouldn't mind being so incredibly old
If it weren't for being so miserably cold.
Wearing this snow cap makes it hard to remember
Whether it's July or the month of December!
I envy the cat with his warm coat of hair,
All cozy and snug in a soft easy chair."

"I love to be cozy," said the comfortable cat,
"But I wish there were something to life besides that:
I stroll through the garden, climb the peach tree,
Take a catnap, and that's the whole day for me!
I wish there were something more exciting to do,
So I could have myself an adventure or two.
To be a small boy would really be great,
A lively young sprite of age seven or eight.

"He can roller skate and ride on a bike,
He can climb a tree and go on a hike,
He can fly a kite and wade in a brook,
He can play football and read a good book,
And that's not all, that's only a few
Of the things a boy is able to do—
The boy is the lucky one, no doubt of that,
If you'll take the word of a silly old cat."